ANTHOLO

FIVE HUNDRED WORDS

COLLECTED STORIES

YSTRADGYNLAIS CREATIVE WRITING GROUP

FOREWORD BY LAZARUS CARPENTER

SWIFT ARROW BOOKS

MORE TITLES FROM

LAZARUS CARPENTER

CRACH FFINNANT – THE PROPHECY

CRACH FFINNANT – RISE OF THE DRAGON

CRACH FFINNANT – RAVENS AND DRAGONS

CRACH FFINNANT – JUSTICE PREVAILS

CRACH FFINNANT – STRONGHOLD OF ILLUSION

WALLS HAVE EARS – ROCK OF THE NIGHT

(The History of Craig y Nos Castle)

HERMIT AND THE DOG WOLF & OTHER STORIES

BALLAD OF PENYGRAIG

FIVE HUNDRED WORDS

COLLECTED STORIES

VOLUME ONE

YSTRADGYNLAIS CREATIVE WRITING GROUP

Copyright © 2023 by Lazarus Carpenter

All rights reserved. This book or any portion thereof may not be reproduced or used in any manner whatsoever without the express written permission of the publisher except for the use of brief quotations in a book review or scholarly journal.

First Printing: 2023

ISBN <978-1-4477-2069-0>

SWIFT ARROW BOOKS Ltd

107 Cyfyng Road, Ystalyfera, Swansea, Wales. SA9 2BT

www.lazaruscarpenterauthor.com

www.swiftarrowbooks.co.uk

Ordering Information:

Special discounts are available on quantity purchases by corporations, associations, educators, and others. For details, contact the publisher at the above listed address.

CONTENTS

Dedication	11
Acknowledgements	12
Foreword	13
Chapter 1	15
Chapter 2	30
Chapter 3	48
Chapter 4	64
Chapter 5	73
Chapter 6	86
Chapter 7	95
Chapter 8	103
Chapter 9	107
Chapter 10	117
Chapter 11	121
Chapter 12	130
Images	139
Storytellers	141

Lazarus Carpenter
Creative Writing Group Facilitator

DEDICATION

Storytelling originated with visual stories, such as cave drawings, and then shifted to oral traditions, in which stories were passed down from generation to generation by word of mouth. There was then a shift to words formed into narratives, including written, printed and typed stories.

This book is dedicated to all storytellers who have walked the earth from the beginning of time, and into our future.

ACKNOWLEDGEMENTS

Grateful thanks to Powys County Council, Ystradgynlais Library, manager, and staff for use of the meeting room facilities.

We would also like to express sincere gratitude to the members of the Creative Writing Group who contributed to this book with their stories, Matthew and Rosalyn Gough, Ade and Jane Levi, Meiriona Davies, Jay Sacher, Jo Paine, Gill Opal, Paula Jardim, and Holly Morgan.

Finally, grateful thanks to the Creative Writing Group's facilitator, award winning author, Lazarus Carpenter for hosting the *creative space,* and organizing the publishing of this Anthology of Collected stories.

FOREWORD

It has been an absolute pleasure and honour to facilitate the Creative Writing Group every week. Over the months, membership has increased bringing yet more talented folk with their individual unique imaginations. No two stories are the same, yet all are imagined from one image in each chapter. Their short stories are printed in this collected works.

Creating a story limited to *five hundred words* is no easy task but there are sound reasons behind the weekly exercises. Storytelling is a skill which if honed, and directed can result in stunning portrayals with words, and images leaping from a page like a mini film. Each week the group shared an image then in their own time, wrote a story to reflect their ideas about how the picture spoke to them.

The completed stories though limited to *five hundred words*, excludes the word count of a title. Many writers have issues about keeping a story on track as ideas keep coming to mind during the creative process, and blurring an intended storyline. Initially, this exercise assisted members of the group to stay on track with their stories, moreover, to spark an intuitive drive.

In the beginning I was not overly concerned about spelling, punctuation or the finery of presentation, these things can be learned easily, good storytelling cannot. So directing the writers to limit their word count for a story encouraged them to be careful around structure whilst maintaining an emphasis on an intuitive theme. My only guidelines were to study the image, leave it alone for a few minutes perhaps whilst having a coffee, then revisit it, close one's eyes, and then write everything coming to mind stimulated through intuitive thought.

When folk were happy with their story it would be emailed to me for viewing, formatting and editing. In the early days there was a lot of editing offered, and there would be learning points to share with the writers. At the next meeting of the group, members read their story out loud in order to encourage feedback which in turn slowly increased their confidence with storytelling.

The publication of this collected works is intended to increase their confidence as writers even further. Nothing is finer for a storyteller than to see their tale, and name in a book. Our writers have achieved this, and it is with pleasure and baited-breath I await more stories, and possibly even novels from them. I hope you as a reader enjoy the tales as much as I enjoyed witnessing their growth as storytellers.

Lazarus Carpenter

CHAPTER ONE

Image One
Story One

The Violin Player

    The old man sat alone in his dark room surrounded by the few treasured possessions of his life. The most treasured was his violin which he kept in an old sack bag

tied with string. The violin was a possession from his youth, as a member of an orchestra.

    As he tried to remember the tunes of his youth he would dream of the days when he played to the villagers at the local dances

11

and his spirit would lift as he recalled those days. He had met his sweetheart who became his wife and they had settled into a happy life together with the old man teaching at the village school. Today though, darker thoughts played on his mind as he recalled the sounds of gunfire and the war cry of young men amongst the stench of mud and blood of the trenches

The old Man had lost his most treasured loves, not only his wife and a young son, but many of his young comrades, but he had his violin and just holding it close brought him such comfort. He dearly wished he could recollect the tunes he had played. His hands were crippled with arthritis, he could no longer reach the cords as easily as he wished. The summer evening was warm, and the fading sun beckoned to him as the light from the window played upon his bent head. But still he sat with a determination to remember the music.

Sometimes a walk could refresh his memory and he would hurry back home quickly taking off his coat and hat and grab his violin. His neighbors would smile as they passed listening to the strained notes of the violin. They had known him as a younger man with wife and child. The war had led both Father and son to enlist, the father as a musician and the son barely out of his teens as a fighting soldier.

The old man had joined a regiment where the officer in charge of the entertainment troops recognized music as an emotional link between home and the front and would summon the musicians together when there was a lull in the fighting. The old man would pick up his violin and with his comrade's play the favorite tunes of the day. The troops would join in singing remembering their families and sweethearts at home.

It was a day in late summer 1918, when he received news of his Sons death. He had been playing his violin in the field hospital where medics and patients alike would listen to the soft tones of his violin. He had learnt that his son had died from a sniper's bullet in attempting to rescue a young private. Today was the anniversary of his son's death and in a moment of extreme grief he looked up at his sons' picture on the wall vowing to play his one last piece of music in his son's memory.

Rosalind Gough

Story Two

Bertie's Song

Sitting in his room Bert picked up the violin and bow. For the time he played the maelstrom in his mind calmed. So pure was the clarity that the air was no longer filled with polluted thoughts and memories. The fragments of a life he believed belonged to someone or somewhere else no longer existed. He felt like a bird on a summer's morning, alive and vivid.

Elsie Fitch knocked on the door daily and left a pot with either some stew or porridge. They never spoke, she referred to him as 'that poor sod' – she heard the nights he cried out, the times he crawled around the room on his hands and knees trying to hide under the furniture, the sobbing, begging it to stop.

The trenches where men shouted, the reek of decaying flesh, gunpowder and excrement. A vain attempt at humor, a smoke between pals, until they were told to 'fix bayonets', all banter stopped. The relentless thumping of the shells, they were being peppered with mud and stones, pinging off their tin hats, from the approaching army. Whistles blowing scrabbling over the top to be cut down like a scythe cutting through grass. Taffy next to him, legs blown off, and his torso catapulted through the air, bouncing on landing, a fixed grimace on his contorted face. One of hundreds of thousands who lost their lives on the fields of terror, where today poppies bow their heads to each and every one.

Bert couldn't remember how he came to be in this room, his leg full of shrapnel. He must have been stretchered off the field and taken to a makeshift hospital. He heard the voice of a girl 'now Bertie we're going to fix you up and get you home'. Her touch was kind as she wiped his brow. She wasn't caked with clay nor had a face blackened with charcoal ready for battle.' She wore a crisp white uniform her clean shiny hair worn in a bun. When the Colonel of the regiment visited he put his hand on Bert's shoulder 'dam lucky you are old chap, dam lucky, there's, he a lot worse off than you Harman' turning on his heels, that was the end it seemed to Corporal Albert Harman's battle but it truth it had really just begun.

One February afternoon a milky sun shining through the only window, there was a soft tap on the door. On opening a women stood in a navy wool coat, she had soft brown eyes and neat auburn hair. Behind her Mrs. Fitch and a man dressed in a pinstripe suit holding a clipboard.

'It's me, Dad, its Alison, your daughter'.

Bert searched her eyes looking for something to say,

'Don't worry Dad, you're coming with me, the buildings been condemned.

I'll come back next week. We've got a house in Bexley Heath Dad, with a lovely sunny room overlooking the garden for you. You can play your violin to your heart's content'.

Jo Paine

LAZARUS CARPENTER

Story Three

Sounds from a Violin

Gerald, was standing very still in the cold air at Ypres. As a trained Doctor and trauma surgeon he was taking a quick break. The stink from the trenches was startling, noxious warfare gas mixed with gunpowder fumes numbed the mind. But the bravery of men was overwhelming. This was no ordinary night, the shelling and explosions, dreadful sounds so loud it numbed the senses. Between the trenches Gerald, heard a terrible scream for help, and jumped out of the trench to offer assistance. In the mist he caught sight of a badly injured German soldier. Gerald administered morphine, but it was too late for anything else. The dying soldier passed Gerald a violin from under his greatcoat. With final gasps of breath, in broken English he stuttered.

'A present for you my friend.'

Gerald closed the soldier's eyes and carefully hid the violin under his greatcoat. Time passed and the war came to an end. Gerald returned to London after the war where he became a brilliant surgeon saving many lives, married his partner and together they had three children. His life was dedicated to medicine and his family. The years passed by and were kind to Gerald, but before he knew it retirement arrived. He had many grand memories but was still haunted in nightly dreams by the horror of the trenches.

As World War II progressed Gerald reflected on the pains of war. Outside the house in the street he could hear a group of children singing, it was Christmas Eve and suddenly he remembered the violin. He was unable to play nowadays due to arthritis, or so he thought. The snow fell like a huge white curtain covering everything outside like a blanket, and he could see and hear the children singing Christmas carols. Gerald picked up the violin thinking to himself, *perhaps it was time for a tune.*

Suddenly something remarkable happened, he felt the arthritis easing. Holding the bow and violin he played along accompanying the children's singing. He wasn't sure if it was him playing the violin, or the violin was playing itself. The children loved his playing and a number of people passing by stopped to listen. Gerald blinked twice, for on the horizon there was a ghostly man standing in a muddy greatcoat smiling. It was a young man seemingly looking like the soldier Gerald tried to save during World War I. The singing and playing continued, but within a blink of an eye, the ghostly young man was gone.

Gerald was taken aback by the apparition, but carried on beautifully bowing the violin with ease. The children continued singing accompanied by his incredible playing. When they finished Gerald gifted the violin to a young lad conducting the choir.

He returned to his apartment feeling very happy within himself. The boy grew to a man, and all through the Second World War entertained the troops with his beautiful music. After the war he had a successful career in the music halls.

Matthew Gough

Story Four

Adam

In a dilapidated house, an old man sat upon a wooden chair. His elbow leaning on the armrest helped to support the neck of a violin cradled in his left hand; the chinrest leaning clumsily on an arthritic knee. A gnarled hand lay on his knee helping control the shaking thumb, index finger grasping the eye of an old violin bow. Tired eyes stared vaguely at the tip of his violin bow the end of which, lightly touched a dusty wooden floor, a quiet mind no longer remembering who he once was.

Silently and motionlessly time stood still for this old man. Grains of dust colored the oil lamp, dim light lazily dancing on a sooty table. In silence the living spirit of a colorless portrait on the wall behind his stooped shoulders whispered tales from times long gone, forgotten stories weighing heavily on curved aching shoulders. Adam was his name. His musty brown slippers and thick socks failing to warm ageing feet, an addled mind hiding a thousand tales of war, peace, and forgotten love.

On occasions his fingers would stroke the violin, which in gratitude for the received caresses would gift him back musical memories from yesteryear. Images drifting to mind, fragments of his childhood, of time serving in the army, of intoxicating secret affairs, fleeting images of love, loss, grief and sorrow; seen now from a distance experienced as if they belonged to someone else. Sitting on the dusty chair old Adam's mind having lost his sense of 'I', rested peacefully in open awareness. Hard of hearing, he was no longer able to hear the lonesome cries of his old self, forgotten on the crumbling wall.

"What about me?" Implored the disconsolate picture. "Can't you see, I am still here, still alive, can't you see I don't want to die?"

Oblivious, Adam, sat perfectly still. Desolate in isolation the portrait hanging on the crumbling wall began to cry, silent tears falling on the pencil marks, drip by drip, finally dissolving into a discolored smudge as the grandfather clock struck midnight. At that precise moment the heavens cracked open and the earth shook violently. The framed picture fell off the wall and the old man dropped his violin on the floor as the sound of shattered glass jolted him from the chair. Slipping on the violin bow Adam, fell onto the floor slashing himself with broken glass, and began bleeding profusely from the wounds. As the blood began to spread across the floorboards, and as each droplet reached a broken piece of the framed portrait, the blood began gathering and reassembled creating a crystal glass goblet.

When the rescue team arrived at the earthquake scene, sounds of a violin could be heard playing amongst the rubble. Seeking the mysterious tune, they found a jewel-encrusted cup. Legend says that when caressed, the mysterious crystal cup miraculously fills with medicinal wine and plays a melody capable of healing those who hold it from the suffering of ageing, sickness and death.

Paula Jardim

Story Five

The Violin

In 1904, Albert, was eight years old. Every Saturday, was market day and like clockwork he accompanied dear mother, shopping for the weekly groceries. Albert looked forward to standing by the entrance to the market again, to be mesmerized by sweet gentle tones bowed by an old man playing a battered violin. He watched how he held the bow, and tucked his violin so neatly under a whiskered chin. The old man played so beautifully and every week was the same, his mother would take his hand gently pulling him away. Nothing could stand in the way of the weekly shop.

Albert longed for a violin of his own, but he knew times were hard and money was short. On Christmas day he rushed downstairs, his face lighting up in delight, as there under the Christmas tree was a present wrapped in newspaper with his name on. Anxious to see what it could be, he carefully unwrapped the newspaper.

'A violin.' He gasped in joy and excitement.

This was his very first violin albeit more of a toy, it still had catgut strings and a wooden bow. All the same Albert, was delighted and he took the bow in his right hand, placing the violin under his chin with the other. He plucked the catgut strings one by one with tiny fingers.

Two years later on Christmas day Albert, reached his twelfth birthday and on Christmas morning he rushed downstairs to find a somewhat more colorfully wrapped present, a blue silk ribbon bow tied fittingly on top. He unwrapped the parcel with excitement and in utmost surprise screamed.

'Mum, Dad, a real violin, a real one. Thank you, thank you.' He kissed them both fondly.

Albert's mother decided to arrange lessons for him with the violinist who played in the market. After many a lesson

Albert, achieved much over his younger years and became an accomplished violinist. The years passed by and in 1914 war broke out. Albert, enlisted into the army at eighteen and trained as a medical officer, sailing off to war in France.

The war was fierce and bloody. Soldiers fighting battle in the trenches, or on the field were inflicted with awful wounds and thousands were killed. Albert spent his days in the trenches, tending the terrible wounds of his comrades in arms. To ease their anxieties, pain and sorrow, Albert would take his violin and bow soothing dulcet tones, playing on and on.

Many years passed and Albert, now in his twilight years often stared at a photograph on the wall. He was alone with memories, the pain of great sadness and the atrocities of war. Sitting for many hours alone in a humble home playing the ageing old violin, tears would fill his eyes and yet still he played on and on.

The memories would always live on, never would he forget his beloved comrades and friends no longer here. It was Albert's way, the only way of easing his broken heart.

Jane Levi

CHAPTER TWO

Image Two
Story One

No Going Back

 Standing at the bar, hand outstretched ready to lift a pint glass, George the barman served him, he could not help but hear chatter from the men behind. Gambling with cards round the old black stove standing in the middle of the room, a daily occurrence, seemingly forever. Calling him to come and join them, he nodded, implying, *'shortly'*. Staring into the pint, froth swirled round, as he felt his being pulled and drawn down and down. Memories came flooding back, happenings from the past. Casting his mind back remembering, Mary, his beautiful, loving, caring Mary, who he ill-treated over their 40 year marriage.

She stood smiling at him as she always did. *'God'* He thought. *'Why had he treated her so badly? And the four children she had borne him? Why?'* A tear dripped into the corner of his eye, falling down an unshaven chin.

He was no use to her and reminded himself of when they lost their youngest child Charlie, to pneumonia in 1924. He remembered going off to the pub to drown his sorrows, while Mary was left alone at home comforting their other three children. A task he should have done, whilst she rested. There was Betsy, the barmaid whom he had a dalliance with for a few years, but Mary never chastised him. *'Guilt, Good God, guilt.'* something he never felt in his life surged through him now. Swallowing hard, he felt a lump in his throat. Elbow still on the bar, with an open hand suspended over the pint glass, the swirling froth called him back, memories surging.

Now, the child he once was with clear blue eyes, blond curly hair, and a boy everyone admired. Even when beastly towards his two elder sisters and stealing their sweets, he was never chastised. His mam would just click her tongue and look disapprovingly, with a hint of a smile. His sisters were always tolerant of him and his temper tantrums. His dad was less tolerant, making him learn jobs on the farm. When he grew up he worked in the colliery.

Oh yes, he always worked hard, and at the tender age of nineteen, fell in love with Mary, married three years later, and went on to have four children. But their marriage was ruined by his foul temper, even though Mary always found excuses for his bad behavior. He began to drink heavily and was off out boozing and gambling with his mates, leaving Mary to look after the children, and the farm.

Feeling a tug at his leg, there looking up with velvety brown eyes was Meg, his faithful Border collie dog. Yes, he had seen eyes like this before, and ignored their love shining out like beacons.

Having walked through 40 years being cocksure to only now realize, what he had thrown away. Lifting his elbow from the bar he spat in the spittoon. Leaving the pub, pint untouched he walked home with Meg to an empty farmhouse.

Meiriona Davies

Story Two

Travelling Man

Jack Trodd finished his beer with a sour grimace. He had been stood at the bar for long enough and it was time for him to move on. His Staffie dog had been lying patiently at his feet but now stood waiting, sensing before his owner did, it was time to go. The weather outside was bitter and Jack was reluctant to step over the threshold. He had no particular place to go, since his wife Betty passed three months ago Jack felt he had lost the last solid thing in his life. Jack and Betty had been together since their mid-teens, and he smiled at the many good memories emanating from shared decades. Undoubtedly there had been hard times, all part of the life they were both been born into.

Romany life was hard but made harder by the prejudice and intolerance coming from Gorjas, those who lived settled lives in houses. But the strong shared sense of family ties and tradition insulated them from much of that. Anyway that was how it had always been, a grim kind of acceptance of them and us further softening the blows.

Jack remembered evenings around the fire, songs and stories shared, banter about the day's work they found in the area. That unspoken rich pride of tradition going back generations. Throughout their lives Betty and he watched their way of living, squeezed out more and more. Roads becoming faster, park ups disappearing behind bollards and fences. Young policemen with court paperwork and unfeeling faces demanding them to move on. Places where they had always stopped to pick the local fruit or harvest hops now gone, to be replaced by fast food outlets and out-of-town shopping centers.

'Settle onto the site that we've provided for you.' came the refrain.

All Jack recalled from these sites was they stank from the nearby sewage works or recycling centers. The children would develop coughs and the flies in the summer were intolerable. He wouldn't keep a dog in those places. Gradually the travelling group was broken up until now it was just Jack on his own. With a sigh Jack pushed open the door of the pub, too much thinking about the past was not good for him. Better to move on towards something good. Yes, he would go on up and stop in on his brother Joe. Joe had done alright in finding a place, even if the rumble of the motorway was a constant in the background. Joe's wife, Sarah, and their children would be good company for a while.

They seemed happy enough, settled in their own way but still holding Romany threads in everyday lives. Greeting the patient piebald cob tethered outside, Jack climbed up onto the wooden step of the brightly colored barrel topped wagon, his dog hopped up beside him settling comfortably on his old blanket bed. Flicking the reins Jack set off moving on, as he always had done and always would do until the day he finally ran out of road for the last time.

Jay Sacher

Story Three

Spirits

Ye Olde Oak Inn, stood quaintly amongst towering fir trees surrounded by a small forest. Inside oak beams are clustered with horse brasses, copper jugs and ancient memorabilia displayed on iron hooks. An old stone fireplace glowed in the corner. Suddenly the door opened and in walked an elderly gentleman.

'You do know there are spirits here?' He asked the landlord rhetorically.

'We have many spirits here Sir, brandy, rum, whiskey.' The landlord gave a knowing look.

'I have heard tales of creaking floorboards, door handles turning, and visitations of phantom ghosts walking upstairs.' Added the old gentleman.

'I do not believe in those sort of goings on, nothing occurred here, that I do know.' The landlord pulled a pint.

The elderly man supped another ale and sat beside the fire. That same evening a young couple arrived looking for a room. The landlord booked them in, collected the suitcases and climbed a narrow staircase showing them to the room.

'Evening meal is at 7pm, breakfast at 8am.' The landlord disappeared down the corridor.

After a good dinner they joined the elderly gentleman in the lounge, taking a small settee by the fire. After a while feeling tired they went to their room. Wind howling, torrential rain and claps of thunder exploded outside, but they managed to drift off to sleep. Suddenly they awoke with a start as the door handle turned slowly left then right. The young woman screamed.

'Did you see that? I am scared, why is the door handle turning, why?'

Her husband felt fearful and got out of bed to investigate. Nothing at all could be seen and eventually they returned to sleep.

At three he woke again startled and shook her shoulder.
'Wake up, wake up now.'
'What, what?' She rubbed tired eyes.
'Creaking outside in the corridor.' He stuttered.
'Sleep.' She said closing her eyes.

Next morning they ate breakfast and told the landlord what happened. He just laughed not believing one word. Their second night turned out to be just as eventful, again the turning door handle, the creaking of the corridor floor. This time they both investigated the strange happenings. As they opened the bedroom door, a vivid light of a ghostly figure confronted them, hovering at the top of the winding stairs.

The following morning, packing their suitcase, rushing down the stairs and refusing breakfast they bade farewell to the landlord, leaving the door closed behind them. Driving along country lanes and arriving at the next village, they decided to stop at a small coffee shop and order breakfast. A waitress served them with a smile. They told her all about their frightening two nights at the inn. Suddenly her smile disappeared and with a look of concern shadowing her face she announced.

'Ye Olde Oak Inn has not been inhabited for very many years, not since the landlord and an elderly gentleman sadly died in a fire from embers falling onto the floor. You see, they were the ghosts.'

Jane Levi

Story Four

The Glass is Half Full

Up on the tor wisps of dense fog swirled and froze against the gorse, portraying ghost like shapes along the path. Between swirls of fog, the moon shone with an iridescent silvery light, intermittently obscured by fleeting fog. The outline of a man with a four legged friend walked along the lane towards the pub on the hill. As he entered a glass of beer was waiting for him on the bar. Lulu the greyhound also lay in wait, she was great friends with the man's dog.

This night was different, the man was shedding a quiet tear. Now he is without family, they don't even know where he is and perhaps did not even care, they left long ago. The dog looked up mournfully at the man with sad eyes. A bright light shone above the man's head, a kind of shimmering orb. He turned to his dog and said.

'Do not worry my time on this planet is coming to an end.' he took the dogs paw, in an act of communication and love.

They shared such lovely memories and warmth, the dog in turn looked straight into the man's eyes with such love and compassion. He reassured the dog by saying.

'Look for me when least expected, I will be keeping watch over your life and protecting you to the best of my ability from heaven.'

The greyhound moved even closer, sharing and giving warmth. The glow from the orb embraced them both and with that, the man's spirit was gone and headed to the stars, with a little twinkle. This is all we know of this tale. The greyhound invited the dog into his pub and they both had a lovely time, much to the occasional annoyance of the bar manager. They shared a comfortable warm place by the fire in winter months and often, both would see the old man, smiling and surrounding them in good cheer. The man had such a sad life, and really loved dogs more than people. He always tried to do well in the world and be kind to everybody, but the world would not always return the favor. His house he called home fell into disrepair, but gave a lovely silhouette against the silvery moon. The dogs had a great life in the pub and the landlady would often ask herself, '*was this man's glass half full, or empty?*'

The landlady found a letter from him and as she opened it, out shone a shaft of light embracing her with great warmth and love. Coming from a man who truly loved his dogs, the landlady felt the glass was half full. She placed the empty glass on the shelf in honour of the man with a warm heart, who despite everything shared a lot of kindness. When the house was finally pulled down, several thousand pounds was discovered. A dog kennel was built on the site, as instructed by the man.

Matthew Gough

Story Five

Fourteen Years

First Year

Have you ever heard the quote? *Be careful what you wish for.* Rodger Wilson hadn't. All his life he could not find someone to love, and love him in return. In his teenage days, yes, he enjoyed a fair number of girlfriends, and some fell for him whilst others didn't. Never did he experience one spark of affection. He watched his friends have steady relationships getting married, and starting a family. He wanted that too, he needed to feel, and he wanted to love. Every night kneeling he prayed for a woman to come into his life, fall in love, and grow old with each other. By the time his thirty-fifth birthday arrived, he started giving up.

One day a knocking on the door. Nobody there but a large box sat on the doorstep. *Strange* he thought, and bending down to pick up the box he almost dropped it. Something inside moved and a faint whining came from within. Roger carried the box inside, and opened it. There sat a puppy with two tins of dog food, but no note. He lifted the puppy from the box, opened a tin, and spooned dog food into a bowl.

Second Year

The puppy grew into a fine looking dog, a Shetland sheepdog. Rodger named her Shetty, and took her everywhere, to the pub, long walks in the park, along riverbanks, wherever he went, she went.

Third Year

One morning while shaving Rodger, thought he looked much older than his thirty-eight years, seemingly closer to forty-eight. His eyes had bags under them, his skin was wrinkly, and his thinning hair greying around the temples. How had he failed to notice these changes before?

'What shall we do today Shet?' he asked the dog. 'How about

we go to the beach, and see if we can spot a few lovely ladies?'

As usual, not one woman caught his attention. Many were pretty, great figures, but that was all. He saw Shetty sniffing at something near the water's edge.

'Shetty, away from there now!' he called.

She gave a yelp, staggered and then vomited. Rodger ran towards her and saw the reason. It was a jellyfish. Shetty began to tremble so he lifted her into his arms. It was a good job he was fit enough, those daily exercises had paid off. He sobbed uncontrollably running toward the car with her cradled in his arms.

Don't die.' he pleaded, 'I love you so much. Just hold on, hold on!'

Fourteenth Year

It was Rodger's forty-ninth birthday. Riddled with arthritis he needed a stick to walk nowadays. His body was that of an eighty year old. Shetty having survived her encounter with the jellyfish, was almost the same age in dog-years. Today they are going for a walk to the pub, maybe for the final time. Rodger stood at the bar holding a glass between arthritic fingers sipping beer.

Well, I got what I wished for, a female to love and grow old with.

Ade Levi

Story Six

Cadan

Thwack! The only sound heard on a quiet still evening. A man fell lifelessly to the cobbled street staining with thick dark red blood mingling with the soft Cornish rain. Cadan woke with wife Tamsyn beside him. The simple room had white-washed walls, wooden cross above the bed, and a wash stand in the corner. Tamsyn was a 'bal maiden' working above ground at the tin mine, whilst Cadan worked below.

For a year he wooed Tamsyn, but she stuck with her twin sister Maisy, and the other women who were a fierce breed breaking rocks for a living. One mid-summer's day Tamsyn, agreed to walk back to the village with him. They sat in a meadow together under the sun staring at a turquoise sea. His love for her grew as deep as the ocean. Married two weeks later they have never spent a day apart. Downstairs in the cob cottage shared for 60 years Tamsyn, hummed softly as she raked out the oven-range. Cadan appeared through the back door.

'Got some dry wood ere my lovely.' a bundle of wood and sticks clattered on the hearth.

'They look just the job.' she said.

Cadan set off for his daily pint to the Ship Inn with Brock. Brock stopped to cock a leg up the wheel of a cart, and sniffed the air when passing the butchers. The dog seemed spooked hesitating as they crossed the path.

'C'mon boy!' encouraged Cadan.

The barmaid asked. 'Usual Cadan?' she pulled dark golden liquid filling a pewter tankard. 'You eard Ned Soames, was found down Trelan path this morn, his ead cracked open?'

'Didn't know 'ee were back round these parts.' Cadan replied. 'Can't say ee would be welcomed by many.'

Cadan, quaffed his pint while beneath him Brock, looked at his master head resting on front legs with sad doleful eyes staring upward. Tamsyn, stood with the range door open. Picking up a short stout stick with a sticky ruby gleam at one end, she slung it on the fire without a thought. Pulling a shawl tighter around thin shoulders she gathered the needlework holding it closer to her face. Suddenly a knock on the door startled Tamsyn.

'Ello Simon!' a policeman stooped speaking through a low beamed door. 'Come in.' she said.

'Sorry Tamsyn, I's got be asking everyone if you heard anything last night?'

Tamsyn, shook her head.

'Well you take good care now. I'll be calling in on you both very soon.'

Later that night they sat on spindle backed wooden chairs either side of the fire. Tamsyn, seemed preoccupied. Cadan, knew her thoughts went back to the day when Maisy, was discovered at the bottom of rocky cliffs, molested body cast away to drown. He knew who done that alright, and promised himself before drawing his last breath, he would see the bugger off! A thin wisp of grey smoke spiraled in the night toward a smiling half-moon where an old man joyfully danced.

Jo Pain

CHAPTER THREE

Image Three
Story One

In the hands of Morpheus

An Alchemist organized his dispensary of shadows, a new batch of laudanum being prepared with a mixture of alcohol, poppies, and herbs to disguise its bitter taste. This was a very strong illicit batch. Mrs. Richards, who used to work as an assistant to the Alchemist awoke barely able to ascertain night from day. She was experiencing stomach cramps and a painful jaw resulting from a previous night's fall. Mrs. Richards thought.

'I must go across the road, I'm in great need of an elixir'.

Wearing her coat, scarf, and slippers she shuffled painfully across the road. Entering the Apothecary she noticed a new bottle of Laudanum waiting on the counter. The Alchemist really didn't like Mrs. Richards, who found out he was cheating patients on medicines dispensed, regularly lacing potions with chalk. In fact he often mused the world would be a better place without Mrs. Richards in it.

'Maybe the extra strength elixir might do the trick?' the Alchemist suggested.

Without a word Mrs. Richards, paid for the medicine, and left the shop shuffling back across the road to her home. Sitting down on her bed she poured a glass of Laudanum. Stomach pains, a very tight chest, and breathing caused her great discomfort. Swallowing the medicine it warmed her body. Mrs. Richards started feeling sleepy, and without a care in the world she fell into the arms of Morpheus. For a very long time, her sleep was disturbed with vivid dreams. Life seemed to be slipping away from Mrs. Richards, she was very cold and clammy.

A very smartly dressed man heard a cry for help as he passed by her window. He entered the house in haste, noticed Mrs. Richards hardly breathing, ashen grey, and comatose. Fortunately he happened to be a physician, and seeing the bottle of Laudanum open with residue splattered everywhere, he suspected poisoning. Helping her to vomit, and drink copious amounts of water Mrs. Richards, left the safe arms of Morpheus returning to a painful world.

'Why are you taking this liquid?' asked the man, 'The potion smells very bitter and strong.'

Mrs. Richards told him the complete story, and of her suspicions about the Laudanum being used as a poison. He called for the police immediately. Three loud knocks at the door of the Apocothery were followed by a number of policemen entering the shop. Ransacking the premises they seized all papers and equipment used by the alchemist. He was arrested and charged with attempted murder, fraud and subsequently found guilty.

She needed a long time to recover however, she eventually became an alchemist too. She treated many ailments but never used Laudanum viewing the substance as very addictive. She helped to develop protective legislation passed into the 1868 pharmacy act which gave better protection to patients. Although the use of Laudanum continued and was used by many clandestine artisans for its psychoactive qualities life was a little safer. As for Morpheus, his arms remain open for souls seeking solace.

Matthew Gough

Story Two

The Old Apothecary Shop

Albert Burtenshaw's Apothecary Shop stood on a quiet back street in a gently run down seaside town. Holidaymakers wandering through to their cheap hotel, sunburnt, and giddy from a day drinking the sun would walk past the charity shops, bank façade with the sign stating, *'This branch is now permanently closed'*, and the shop selling seaside rock and plastic paraphernalia, never noticing the darkly painted door and, simple shop front that stood between or perhaps before, or after Albert's shop was never seen by ordinary people, their gaze simply slid passed it, the mind registering nothing but everyday thoughts. If you could, and had the inclination to watch the door day in, day out, for a year or more, should you choose, then you would not see a soul step in or out over the threshold. Oh sometimes you might see a strangely dressed whistle player sitting nearby on the pavement playing an old tune in return for a few coins. Or a dozing pony waiting hitched to a tiny, highly-painted cart, *'You don't see that very often nowadays.'* But you would write that off to the flotsam and jetsam that blow through any coastal town around the country.

But that is not to say that old Mr. Burtenshaw's shop lacked business. For folk did come, and purchase what they required very regularly. It was simply that you had to know where to look, and what to say. And on this day, which may be now, or then, or perhaps in a time yet to come, Albert had a very special visitor in his shop.

Eliza-May Williams appeared as a plain, old lady. Her headscarf, long skirted dress, and slightly incongruous slippers would have you barely register her in the street. This was exactly what she wanted you to see, and therefore that is what you did see. And, so now we find ourselves inside the shop; inside looking at myriad shelves through the dust motes swirling slowly in the quiet sunlight filtering from the window. Noticing the creature curled up asleep in the corner that is probably a cat, but could be a monkey, or perhaps even a very small man wearing a fur jacket. You wonder what kind of things might be purchased here.

Well, Eliza-May had come to restock her supplies. She needed salves to heal the hurt of previous generations that dragged itself wounded into dreams, and turned them into nightmares; tinctures made from that last light of happy, sun-filled childhood memories that would sooth the sorrow stricken mind of the dying; drops that would clear the thing seen from the corner of your eye as you walked through the woods at nightfall, and lastly powders that would help you take the road in life that you wished you had.

All this, Albert Burtenshaw weighed, measured and dispensed to Eliza-May, who paid with kindness and regret folded up in notes and coins. Leaving the shop, Eliza-May, stepped back through the doorway to her own time and place. Of which is another tale to be told in a different place.

Jay Sacher

Story Three

Ships in the Night

The red glow from the Apothecary lamp shone into the upstairs window of the house opposite where Mary anxiously paced the bedroom, floor boards creaking with each step she took. It was still early evening, and she was in pain and discomfort again clutching at her stomach. She visited the Apothecary last week for toothache and he prescribed oil of clove, and garlic which had some effect. Now the pain returned accompanied by a raging griping stomach-ache. *What was she to do?* She paced a little more but quietly so as not to disturb her husband, who lay in a drunken stupor across the bed having just returned from a local inn.

Mary tutted glancing at her husband snoring like a farm animal. She crept quietly downstairs in her nightdress and slippers, and slipping on her coat, and headscarf went out into the dark street. Lit only by a full moon, and the red glow of the Apothecary shop opposite, off she staggered. The doorbell rang above her head as she stepped into the scrubbed cleanliness, and herbal smelling reception area of the Apothecary. Mary felt hopeful of a remedy. The brilliance of the colored bottles of red, green, and blue, and the neat array of tiny drawers in the cabinet behind the counter always comforted Mary instilling confidence.

The apothecary smiled sympathetically looking concerned as he questioned Mary.

'Have you tried spearmint leaf or chamomile, very soothing and will help you sleep?'

'Yes.' Mary replied, 'I have but to no avail.'

The apothecary searched his herbal remedies book carefully and then looking at Mary with great concern said.

'I can advise you to try henbane which will relieve your toothache and settle your stomach. I will give you a few grains to take immediately with water, and I will include a further two doses to take over the next two days. But,' he warned, 'Please be careful to take as directed as it is a very potent medicine.'

Mary paid for the remedy, and slipping the papers containing the grains into her coat pocket, she left the shop. When she returned home her husband was still fast asleep. She decided to make herself some tea adding the grains of henbane, and very soon she fell fast asleep in a chair by the fire. Mary woke with a sudden start rubbing her eyes. It was now quite late, and she felt lightheaded almost befuddled. Staring through heavy eyes Mary saw the unwrapped papers of the other henbane doses. Unaware she had already taken one dose she prepared another drink, and unwrapped the grains.

The next morning her husband woke feeling fresh and alert washed, and dressed, and came briskly downstairs whistling a merry tune. On seeing Mary asleep in her chair by the fireside he tutted loudly enough to hopefully wake her. But no, Mary slept on looking peaceful and relaxed and dreaming that she was flying as free as a bird in a cobalt blue sky.

Rosalind Gough

Story Four

Booth's Apothecary

Situated on the corner of Pelham Street, Nottingham, stood Booth's established apothecary. Mr. Booth, the proprietor and his wife Mary, an accomplished forager and herbalist were working late into the night. Mary, earlier in the day, had gathered a small bunch of white poppies. In the center of a long table a bright oil lamp cast its light into the shop providing just enough illumination to work under. They were burning the midnight oil! Behind Mr. Booth, stood a large rustic oak cabinet displaying neatly, and in alphabetical order a variety of herbs, lotions, tinctures, and oils in glass jars. A microscope sits on the bottom shelf. Customers come from far, and wide to purchase his successful remedies.

Mr. Booth's long table included an array of laboratory equipment, a Bunsen burner, glass vials, a pestle and mortar, weighing scales, test tubes, all necessary equipment required to create his compounds.

'What have you brought me?' asked Mr. Booth, 'Now they look interesting.'

Mary explained after foraging that during the afternoon in the forest, she came across a patch of white poppies growing in the woods just outside of town, and collected a small bunch. She also noticed in the center of the perfectly formed white petals an abundance of tiny black seeds. Back at the apothecary, Mary watched with curiosity as Mr. Booth gently peeled the white petals away, and shook the black seeds into the bowl of his weighing scales.

'These are very similar to the ones I have on the shelf for the ease of moderate pain. I am going to add a small amount of sucrose, sodium and hydroxybenzoate. Let's just see what I can come up with.'

He carefully placed the compound mixture with the seeds into a glass vial.

'I'll be upstairs if you need me, I am starting to feel quite cold.' Mary said.

She brewed a tea of chamomile flowers and sipped at the mug as she slowly ambled toward a comfortable chair. About an hour later she heard a cry from downstairs.

'Eureka!'

Mary stood and shuffled toward the door calling down to Mr. Booth.

'Is everything alright?'

'Come down Mary, I've discovered a new medicine and tested it out on Fido.'

Fido was a fifteen year old Yorkshire terrier who was in great pain from arthritis.

'Come quickly!' he urged with excitement.

It was getting colder so Mary draped a scarf over her head, donned a warm coat and shuffled downstairs still in her slippers. Mr. Booth was very excited indeed.

'I've tried this on the dog and he seems livelier and not in as much discomfort as he was. Look how he plays with the ball, he has not had so much pain free energy for a long time. I have just discovered a powerful pain killer.'

The little dog scuttled and hopped round and round the shop floor like a puppy. Many years later the old apothecary was no more, and in its place another shop was built becoming, Boots the Chemists.

Jane Levi

LAZARUS CARPENTER

Story Five

The Love Potion

Wolfgang served the last customer of the day closing the shop. It was early closing in the small Bavarian mountain town. This evening was band practice and afterwards they would all go to the local tavern and drink beer. In the flat above the shop that had been in Wolfgang's family for three generations, he put sausages and potatoes on the stove for supper but his first port of call was the bedroom where his wife Monika lay.

'Your husband is at your service madam.' He said as he kissed her forehead.

'Are we having caviar and smoked fish for supper?' She asked, her clear blue eyes slightly creasing at the corners as she smiled.

'No we are having Weisswurst and potatoes my dear.'

'Oh, well as it is you who is cooking it, no doubt it will be delicious husband.'

By the time their conversation ended she drifted back to sleep. Wolfgang put her small hand back under the covers and pulled the window to, closing the curtains from the advancing darkness. The menfolk of the town were in high spirits as they packed up their instruments and headed off to the bar.

'I think I play better after a beer.' Hans said, clapping his friend Wolfgang on the back.

The comradery continued but Wolfgang ever aware Monika was alone hailed goodbyes to his friends, and walked back through the cobbled streets with only the sound of a dog barking in the distance disturbing the cold clear night air. He put the drops from a vial into a cup of warm milk and took it through.

'The maestro returns! Have you made me a magic potion to cure my ills?' said Monika sitting up and smiling.

'I wish I had a potion that would cure you my love but for now it is the usual concoction.'

It was a subject ever present in Wolfgang's mind, the fact he could not cure his wife. The following day a small elderly woman appeared in the shop, she was certainly not familiar. She thrust a small package into Wolfgang's hand, and said with a thick accent.

'You must try these herbs, dilute them and mix with 50 per cent alcohol and I guarantee that you will witness incredible results.'

She scuttled out of the door down the street. In a quiet moment Wolfgang remembered the herbs, the smell was pungent but not unpleasant. He did as the old woman suggested and ended up with a tincture. That evening and for seven successive days he added five drops to Monika's warm milk. Wednesday came around and as usual Wolfgang went to Band practice. On his return he climbed the stairs and to his amazement Monika was standing in the salon, she was fully dressed. Wolfgang speechless thought he had drank far too much beer.

'The maestro returns and I am ready to dance until dawn.'

Wolfgang rushed and held her in his arms in a state of bewilderment.

'Your wish, is my command madam!'

Jo Paine

CHAPTER FOUR

Image Four
Story One

The Brick

Wilfred the woodcutter gathered a stack of willow branches. He collected wood from a forest of tall oaks, willow and birch trees. Wilfred tied them up into a bundle and slung it over his back. Off he walked to market to sell the bundle to Wanda the Weaver. When he arrived there was no sign of her and asking round the market, no one knew where she was. He saw a tinker's caravan and noticed a gypsy dressed in bright colored clothes standing in the doorway.

'I could use that bundle of willow.' He said. 'I need to weave a basket to keep my bits and bobs in. I don't have any money to pay you.'

'It is okay.' replied Wilfred. 'You can have them.'

'Oh, that's kind of you.' said the tinker. 'Tell you what, for your kindness I have something here that may useful to you'.

He disappeared inside the caravan and after a few short seconds reappeared holding something resembling a box. He handed it to Wilfred and said.

'This brick will give you luck, please take it.'

Wilfred gingerly took the brick thinking to himself.
Okay, I'll humor him. 'Thank you very much.' Wilfred said.

He was about to walk away when the tinker called out.

'Make sure you keep the brick inside your house, not outside.'

Wilfred arrived home and close to the front gate stared at the brick saying to himself. *I've carried this all the way back home, for what?* Thinking the gypsy was slightly eccentric, Wilfred decided to get rid of the brick, and threw it down on the ground just outside his gate. It looked like rain was on the way, heavy storm clouds filled the sky. A couple of hours later at dusk, a heavy torrential downpour rattled fiercely against Wilfred's windows. Behind the garden fence rain splashed on the ground and as the brick became wet, small sparks shot here and there. The brick grew brighter starting to increase in size. Suddenly a blinding light filled the air as the brick's dimensions shuddered growing in every direction.

The next morning Wilfred got up, dressed, ate his usual breakfast of porridge oats washed down with milk, and headed outside to cut and gather more willow to sell. He gasped at what he saw beyond the gate. A stone staircase with thousands of steps rose high into the sky. Cautiously Wilfred, stood on the first stone step then the second. Sure enough the steps were solid. Lifting his eyes upwards, he stared up the stairway and wondered where it led.

Climbing the stairs Wilfred felt moisture on his face from clouds he walked through. When Wilfred reached the summit he saw land he had never seen before and ventured forth. Down on the earth below the day grew warm following the torrential rainfall the evening before. Hot sun dried out all the steps leading to heaven as one by one they disappeared, until only one brick sat alone on the grass.

Ade Levy

Story Two

Stairway to Heaven

There he stood breathless, alone, and just a few steps away from the mountain top. Looking back it became clear just how far he had travelled. This lonesome journey had taken him years, in fact a lifetime. Holding on to a walking stick with trembling hands he felt light headed, and weak at the knees. It was getting dark, and his aching back curved under the weight of this bundle of branches collected along the way, cried out for a break. Dark clouds flew across a darkening sky, the ground still drenched from recent rains.

Chilled to the bone, cracks in his worn out boots made tired feet cold, wet and numb. Without a shelter in sight he dreamt of a resting place for the night or just somewhere to sit, and lean against a wall. Bundled load strapped on an aching back, concerned thoughts flooded his mind. He worried once removed, his body lacked enough strength to put it back on, and losing his only possession brought tears to tired eyes. Lost in invading thoughts he hardly noticed the nearing violet-blue mist until it transformed into a nebulous fog wrapping around him.

A deep sleep came. In a dream world he saw the first steps of a stone stairway, and felt a comfortingwarmth coming from this other-worldly landing. His heart wanted to climb it yet, the heaviness of his load rendered him immobile. Then he heard the sound of a voice coming from upon high.

'Oh you ageing man! Can't you see the weight of those old branches are breaking your back, limiting your view, and making arduous a journey meant to be effortless, and delightful to behold?'

Puzzled, the old man queried.

'Are you suggesting these dry branches are bad for me? They might come in useful one day? I might need them to start a fire or create a handrail to make a clothes rack, or to build a bed?'

'Old man, to you I say untie the knots that attach you to that pile of dead wood.' insisted the voice. 'You don't need to start a fire. You need to burn your attachment to wrong views. You don't need a handrail, you need to see the futility of grasping at things that bring you no happiness. You don't need a clothes rack, you need learn to see beyond appearances. You don't need a bed, you need to awaken the divine within you.'

'But who will I be without my bundle of branches?' muttered the man, shaking to the very core of his being. 'What you call a pile of dead wood is my life, each branch a memory.'

'The choice is yours.' replied the Voice.

The man awakened from his dream still surrounded by a thick fog. Unknotting himself from the load he released his burdensome past, straightened his back, and began to experience the lightness of a *present moment*. In that instant a light appeared in the sky, illuminating a stairway to heaven.

Paula Jardim

Story three

Serendipity

Carys woke feeling exhausted again, the same repetitive dream haunting her sleep. She dreamt she was lugging a big pile of wood up steep old stone steps. Never reaching the top, the sticks tumbled down to a man below then the same sequence repeated over and over again. Downstairs in the kitchen the day began with the usual chaos, twelve year old twin boys eating their cereal at a large pine kitchen table whilst playing with action figures. She was greeted by their mum Lucy.

'Morning Carys, help yourself to toast and coffee. We are running late as usual.'

Lucy dashed round the kitchen with an armful of coats and school bags.

'Come on boys, do get a move on.'

Once alone Carys, sat hugging the coffee. She loved it here at the rectory feeling at home, and safe. The Dickenson's were a kind family, opening their home and hearts to her. Mike was vicar of the Parish and Lucy a part-time locum general practitioner, both being members of a Christian program for recovering addicts. Carys sat behind the till in the shop 'Serendipity' belonging to Mona, a friend of Lucy's. The shop was near the harbour, and it sold crystals, dream catchers, handmade soaps, and various curios. Carys, wore her obligatory leggings, Doc Martins, and oversized stripy jumper. She endlessly picked at the cuffs of the jumper when not chewing her nails. Her nickname was Amy, and she bore a striking resemblance to Ms. Winehouse, even down to the thick black eye liner. Mona bustled in.

'Well, what a morning! You wouldn't think going to the Post Office could take so long. I could have walked to India quicker to get incense sticks. Let's have a coffee.' Mona announced that someone called Ed might pop in later. 'He says he does small whimsical paintings and drawings'.

Carys spent the next hour doodling. She ignored the phone

desperate to stay away from her old life. She had been pulled down a road of drugs, and petty crime most of her life. The same crowd, the same loser boyfriends all happy to see her slumped in a doorway whilst rifling through her pockets for a quid. No not this time. Late afternoon an old jeep pulled up.

'Hello you must be Carys, I'm Ed.' He had a bundle under his arm which he placed on the counter. Carys, froze, the first image was exactly the one seen in her dream. 'You look like you've seen a ghost.'

Glancing up Carys saw Ed, had a broad smile and twinkling eyes.

'I started my art after I got clean, a bit of therapy really.'

'No they are great.' Carys said.

They really were very good, pictures of goblins and toadstools, fairies and unicorns, he was very talented. She was locking the door of 'Serendipity', when a jeep appeared beside her.

'Don't suppose you fancy a drink sometime?' Ed asked with his head cocked to one side.

'Yeah,' she smiled. 'That would be nice.'

Jo Paine

CHAPTER FIVE

Image 5
Story One

Anwen and Her Bible

An ancient stone cottage stood amongst a small hamlet nestled under Cader Idris Mountains where steep craggy precipices stretched into the far distance towards Cardigan Bay. Autumn arrived with a newly chilled air,

and dark clouds hugged the mountain peaks. A warm light shines from one of the cottage windows where Bronwyn dressed in traditional Welsh costume with a tall black hat stood in a small kitchen baking bara-brith and welsh cakes. Her husband

Evan, a farm hand is sitting in front of a hot blazing fire. Their sixteen year old daughter Anwen, having collected eggs from their chicken coup is helping her mother to mix the ingredients together. The family always attended chapel each Sunday morning being devout Christians, and having strong religious beliefs. Anwen who is an avid reader could recite many psalms perfectly during religious instruction at school. Her family was very poor, and a Bible was something they had never been able to afford to buy.

Much to the ministers dismay only a minority of the village congregation attended the chapel. A horse and cart pulled up outside their cottage the following day, and there stood Mrs. Jones, the minister's wife with a willow basket ready to collect her weekly supply of eggs, a few slices of bara-brith, and some freshly baked Welsh cakes.

'Hello Mrs. Jones' Bronwyn acknowledged, 'how are you today?'
'Very well thank you. Is your Anwen at home?' said Mrs. Jones.
'Yes she is, I will call her now.'
As Anwen entered the room, Mrs. Jones announced.
'I have heard how interested you are in reading theBible. Would you like to come over to our parish home? We have a Bible you can read.'
'Oh mother can I?' asked a very excited Anwen.
'Of course you may, thank you Mrs. Jones.'

Excitedly Anwen called at their home, and she is led to the study where she becomes engrossed in reading their Bible, reciting psalms and readings to Mrs. Jones and her minister husband. Anwen read the Bible to them both, and they were astonished as to how well Anwen read it. Anwen studied the Bible for many years to come and became a great influence to those around her with God's spirit giving her insight. Her Bible brought an understanding of the deeper meanings of truth and Christianity.

Eventually in her later years she opened a Sunday school for the village children passing on her Bible knowledge of psalms and readings, always capable and ready to lend a helping hand or speak a helpful word. Love and confidence shown by the congregation to her influenced the good in everyone she met. Anwen was invited to read out loud from her Bible in the chapel because of dedication and devotion to her faith. Eventually the chapel's congregation filled the pews many coming from far and wide to hear Anwen recite psalms and readings from the Bible, always dressed smartly in traditional Welsh costume with long fringed shawl and the tall black hat.

Jane Levi

Story Two

The Trial

'Good morning worm, your Honour.' sneered Salem as she stood in the dock of the old chapel that also served as a court room.

'Salem O'Leary, you stand accused before this court of practicing witchcraft. Do you confess? We have ways to make you talk. How do you plead?' the judge asked.

'I have done no harm to anyone, let me go.' she cried.

Salem recalled the hours before she was caught naked among the standing stones. A large fire blazed, her skin glowing orange in the fire light. Blood from the newly sacrificed cockerel dripped from her chin down onto her bare breasts. Unknowingly, she was witnessed by a dozen eyes in the woods surrounding the stones. Salem O'Leary shook the chains that bound her wrists and ankles.

'Lead the witch to the cellars for the test.' bellowed the court usher.

Salem was led away tripping over the chains as she was half dragged down the steps to the vaults. She heard the judge's voice shouting.

'Thou shall not suffer a witch to live. Whosoever lays with the beast shall surely be put to death.'

'Let me go, let me go.' cried Salem, as two men held her attaching the chains to an overhead hook secured to a domed ceiling.

'He who sacrifices to any God save the Lord only shall be utterly destroyed.' hissed the jailer.

She looked around and saw a brazier full of glowing coals. A bench laden with iron instruments stood near. The torturer walked towards the bench and reached out for a poker thrusting it deep into the fire. Sweat ran down Salem's head stinging her eyes as she looked on in horror watching the torturer carrying the glowing rod towards her.

'Let me go!' Shrieked Salem

'Do you confess witch?' snarled the jailer.

'Let me go!' She growled.

The jailer's eyes widened when he heard the guttural voice of the witch.

'Burn her.' he shouted.

The torturer held the glowing poker up, and tried to place it across her eyes. Instead he unwillingly forced it into the jailer's mouth. The screaming subsided as his mouth and lips boiled from the extreme heat of the poker. He staggered away falling into a heap on the stinking blood-stained floor. Salem's eyes glowed red as a spout of fire erupted from her mouth flying towards the torturer, and at the same time the shackles melted. She stepped away half naked and ascended the stairs leading to the chapel's main room. Another trial had already begun as she approached the judge's bench.

'What is this?' he roared.

She stretched out both arms as flames shot out from her hands. An old man sitting behind began praying out loud. Another man at her back was asleep as she entered but now was wide awake after hearing the screams. The whole building was on fire, flames licking viciously up the wooden pillars holding up the roof. Moments later the chapel collapsed in on itself killing everyone inside including Salem.

Ade Levi

Story Three

Devils Work

I am on my way to visit Bethan Davies, she attends my Chapel. It has been rumored she is practicing witchcraft, and such is the furore that I must act. I have my silver cross against my heart, and utter a prayer under my breath. Inside the Cottage Bethan greets me with a soft smile. There are no obvious signs of witchcraft, bundles of sweet herbs hang from the rafters, and a fire in the grate but no sign of a cauldron. I searched her face for signs of a wart but none were apparent. After taking tea and bara-brith with her I bade my farewell. Other than the fact Bethan is a woman on her own over the age of 40 years, I relax as it does not appear to me she is working for the Devil.

Down the track on the edge of moorland I walked as mist descended, and the air freezes. I shrank back into the hedgerow as a black stallion appeared in front of me, eyes wild, and his ears pinned back in anger. The beast reared time after time striking hooves at my face which I shielded with my arms. I fumbled inside my cloak and managed to grab the large silver cross which I thrust in the air. The horse galloped away into the mist but the smell of evil hung heavily. I hit my own front door running as relief swept over me when I entered my home. I poured a glass of sherry and threw myself into an armchair. I dare not sleep but asked God for strength as I knew the Devil was amongst us.

The following day is the Sabbath, and Bethan attended Chapel as usual dressed in her best cloak. She appeared calm and composed, and sang melodiously. She has always arrived alone, and keeps very little in the way of acquaintances. I am mindful having written my sermon this week addressing the perils of dalliances with evil, and that purity is our salvation. I keep one eye on Bethan as I project my voice with all the force I can muster, she does not flinch or even blink.

At the end of the service as is usual, I thank the congregation as they leave very aware many of them now scurry in haste from the

Chapel, not wishing to cross paths with Bethan. She is one of the last to leave.

'A very fine sermon today Pastor.' she whispered quietly, her smile benign.

'We must be mindful of the work of the devil, we can easily stray down the path of greed, envy and hatred.' I replied clasping my hands together.

As I did so I see the mud on my boots from last evening and fear comes over me. Bethan walked away from the Chapel, and just as she reached the path leading to her Cottage she looked over her shoulder and smiled. A chill descended, the sound of galloping hooves pounding in the distance.

Jo Pain

Story Four

Mega, Proud Woman of Llanbedr

Early one Sunday morning in the small village of Llanbedr, Mega was busy in her garden tending to herbs and flowers. She had lived in the village since a small girl, and in the same cottage near to a rocky outcrop under the Mountains. Mega now lived alone, an elderly spinster in the village where families earned their livings in the slate mines or as tenant farmers in the beautiful Welsh valley. She was a very distinctive woman of character, often seen walking the mountains, and woods dressed in long skirts, and boots with a bag on her back collecting samples of wildflowers from which she made her homemade potions.

Early spring with a slight chill in the air Mega, as was her usual custom prepared for Chapel. She dressed slowly and carefully in a skirt, white blouse and apron. Inspecting her Welsh hat for any signs of dirt or dust she gave it a brisk brushing. Her eyesight worsening over the years restricted outdoor activities as her health deteriorated. A strong determined character she would often scold the village children if they ventured too near her cottage but they would run away all the way home laughing.

Mega decided on a whim to wear a paisley shawl instead of the customary red plaid. She wrapped it carefully around slender shoulders as the shawl larger than usual left deep folds around her body. At last she was ready. Mega, was extremely familiar to the well-worn paths across the hills into the village but difficulty in walking had made the journey much slower of late. A proud and stubborn woman she held herself in high esteem never admitting to frailty of any kind.

The Salem Chapel sat deep within the valley, and she wandered slowly down the pathway leading to a small copse of woodland. She stopped at the edge of the wood to catch breath needing to enter the Chapel in a dignified manner. Mega understood others spoke ill of her but this only resulted in making her haughty, defensive, and superior in appearance, and attitude.

Women living on their own isolated, and independent were often assumed by suspicious folk to be witches. Mega's wandering over hills and mountains were subjected to malicious gossip amongst the village women. Sunday was the one day women could walk freely, usually to Chapel.

Mega entered the chapel where the congregation already on their knees were deep in prayer. The preacher glanced with scorn at Mega's late arrival pausing briefly in his sermon. She placed a hand against the pew, prayer book in hand as she felt her way to the well sat usual hard wooden seat. Children peeked through clasped hands resting on their foreheads to get sideways glances as Mega passed them. Women tutted turning to each other in quiet understanding. None of this bothered Mega ajusting the shawl, deep shadows forming in its pattern adopted a vision akin to the sunlit mountains and valleys of the beautiful magical Welsh countryside.

Rosalind Gough

CHAPTER SIX

Image Six
Story One

An Upright Stone

Dawn was rising at Gorsedd Park, and the early sun's rays were meddling with the upright stone and its stony comrades, hewn from the Preseli hills. These stones have been playing with the sun since Nineteen Fifty-Four.

A Cathedral of Owls and a cacophony of crows barking broke the silence of the early morning with a song- like chorus, the frosty filigree colors danced in the sun as a myriad of little rainbows appeared on the stones. Whilst the dulcet tones of bells rang throughout the park banishing the night, well just for now anyway. A Robin swooped and perched on the stones and broke into song, its whispery breath could be seen against the cold air whilst the Pembroke Dangler came south, snow began to fall heavily covering the stones with a white glistening shroud. People ran through the park to take shelter leaving evidential dinted tracks in the snow behind them.

The chatter of tiny children could be heard, whilst toboggans ran the course of the park, some upturning as they crashed into boulders of hard snow. The flakes of snow flew faster in the wind, whilst wisps of freezing rain tried to reach the sky within a vortex in the wind. The berries on the hedgerow had all but gone, giving way to icy like structure.

Light was eerie and grey, a red kite could be heard looking for its dinner. The stones braced themselves against the wind, which howled between them in ice-chilling melody, voices were audible shivering in the plummeting temperatures. Then there was silence and the blanket of snow covered all the trees which, yielded against the strong wind. Robins could be seen sheltering amongst the stones for solace, a hare peered out through a crack at the snow. Slowly the snow stopped and although the sun peeked out no warmth could be felt. A man walked past and left some bread-crumbs for the sheltering birds. The stones stood strong against the forces of nature providing shelter to wildlife, flora and fauna.

The light was starting to fade and the stars could be seen twinkling between holes in the mist, a flash from a meteor trail made this place truly magical and it was becoming even colder as yet more ice formed on the stones and icicles formed like daggers in the night. As the mist descended the stones took on a ghostly appearance and eventually waned in the fog. The moon cast light and the upright stone looked almost golden, an owl had made its nocturnal home on the stone keeping an eye out for a tasty young rabbit. The church bells mournfully chimed to welcome night and the stones continued to guard the park and provide welcome sanctuary for all who may need it.

Seventy-five year celebrations will soon be organized to praise the stones with music and song. Long may celebrations continue at Gorsedd Park where people, wildlife and stones come together with a little mystery and interludes of music?

Matthew Gough

Story Two

A Grave Misfortune

'Great work guys,' exclaimed Margaret Thatcher sitting in the back seat of a car doing eighty mph. In the seat opposite sat John Major who said.

'It went well. Good job Jimmy on disabling those security cams.'

Jimmy, sitting in the passenger seat replied, 'Was a piece of cake.'

With two hands pinching each side of his neck he peeled a rubber mask away from his head. The mask was the face of Ted Heath. Margaret Thatcher and John Major did the same.

'How far is the cemetery Jack?' asked Mick who was behind the wheel of the blue Focus serving as the getaway car they rode in.

'Bout ten miles,' replied Jack who was the gang's leader.

They had just pulled a very successful bank robbery which took many months of careful planning. Tommy was unusually quiet, and Jack put it down to a case of nerves. They arrived at the destination. Heading for the boot Jack, sprung it open taking out a bolt cutter. He placed the jaws on the padlock holding the gate shut. Tommy, Mick, and Jimmy hauled out the rucksacks that held two million pounds in notes. They carried the bags through the cemetery gates following Jack into the dark graveyard. A stone building stood in front of them, it was Jack's great grandfather's mausoleum. Earlier that day Jack cleared his ancestor's remains to make room for the sacks of money. It took all three of them to lift the heavy stone slab. Placing the sacks into the tomb they lowered the heavy lid back into place.

'Remember guys six months, and we will be rich. Until then it stays here.' Jack emphasized caution.

Later in the week Jack, sat in his kitchen drinking decaf and reading the Sunday Sport. They were in the clear or so it seemed. *Two million smackers, and all mine.* He reached out in front of him taking hold of a pistol with a silencer attached. He placed into a holster strapped to his shoulder. Getting up out of the chair putting on his coat he left the flat. Mick, Tommy, and Jimmy sat around a table in Mick's house playing poker when the front door bell rang. Mick got up and went to see who it was.

'What's that?' asked Tommy hearing a dull thump in the hallway.

Jack entered the lounge, and shot Jimmy between the eyes. He turned the gun on Tommy and fired, leaving the house via the back door. Using a crowbar Jack, pried the heavy slab placing a brick in the gap repeating the process five times. Torch in hand he shone it into the tomb. Unsure where the stash was he leaned in. There was nothing to be seen. Behind him he heard something moving, a whooshing sound as something heavy smashed into the bricks. The slab fell down onto his head, and killed him instantly. Tommy, a bandage covering his ruined ear holding a sledgehammer smiled walking away.

Jane Levi

Story Three

Ancient Secrets

'Can we hear about great Uncle Robert mummy?'

My two young sons sat in bed often asking to hear this tale as their bedtime story. At five and seven years it created a source of wonderment and awe.

'My great Uncle Robert Spencer was an archaeologist in the 1920's. He and a small team from England went to Egypt to explore the tombs in the pyramids. Over one hundred and eighteen pyramids were built housing burial chambers of Kings, called pharaohs who it was believed after death started a journey in another world. The pharaoh's were placed deep inside the pyramids in ornate stone coffins called sarcophagi.

They were buried with everything needed for the afterlife such as tools, food, wine, perfume, and often even their servants. But it was their valuables which were in such demand. The richer a pharaoh the more gold, and jewels were placed inside around their mummified bodies as it was believed it would lead to wealth, and comfort in the next world, the afterlife. Gold held huge significance to their sun God, Ra. Many of these tombs have been raided over the centuries but there was still so much to learn, and extraordinary discoveries were still being made.'

Robert slept in freezing temperatures at night in tents under the stars having eaten great platters of rice with almonds, and lamb provided by the locals. On special occasions they were served brains with eyes considered a delicacy. At first light before the blistering heat of day the expedition set off to the pyramids mounted on a camel train. The great beasts never seemed to eat or drink but hissed and spat, and were the only form of transport. The pyramid was over three hundred feet high, and inside the entrance daylight disappeared as they entered a labyrinth of tiny passages leading to secret chambers where hours of painstaking work began. Sandy dust was inhaled with every breath, and eerie shadows appeared on the ancient stone walls cast from lanterns. Robert heard echo's from inaccessible passages of children's cries, and weird scraping sounds above him.

When they returned to London all were hailed as heroes. Robert wrote scientific papers and was invited to give lectures illustrated by grainy black and white photographs. They bought back amulets, and items from the tombs which were displayed. Such was the fascination at the time mythical stories circulated told in darkened rooms about the fate of those who entered the tombs. Morpheus embraced them as I tucked both my sons in, and turning out the light I hesitated at the door wondering if I would ever tell them the real end to the story of my Great Uncle. Robert did return to London and married his fiancé Elizabeth. Now considered to be an eminent archaeologist he went to the African continent to discover stone circles. One morning the grizzly mauled bodies of he, Elizabeth, and their young children were found. Wounds inflicted by a creature no local had ever seen.

Jo Paine

CHAPTER SEVEN

Image Seven
Story One

Matilda the Duck and Friends.

It was a lovely morning in summer and on the farm activities were like most days. The farmer was repairing a farmyard shed, and his wife was scattering feed for the ducks, hens, and geese. Of course

68

there was fresh water for all. Matilda thought, *what an idyllic life. Or was it?*

Strange things happen, thought Matilda, *some of my friends simply disappear, without any trace, not a fox in sight or evidence of feathers on the ground and sometimes new acquaintances join the clan. But why do these things happen?* Matilda wondered. *Sometimes a horse drawn trailer with boxes on it, turns up and then my friends are put in the boxes and disappear without trace. Our eggs vanish every day and according to the hens this can't go on, life is unreal. I must have a chat with my friends Bertie the farmyard dog and Sam the Badger.*

That evening Matilda asked her friends to join her for a talk, before they were locked in the shed for the night. The consensus was something terrible was going on. Bertie told Matilda what he knew to be true.

'You guys in the barn are a convenience, eggs are harvested, and your friends are slaughtered for food. New stock arrives to keep the cycle going.'

'Will you help us?' asked Matilda, 'we need to escape.'

'Yes of course. Over the next field there is a peaceful lake where visitors feed others like you, and a warden looks after everyone.'

'Can we organize an escape in two days?' Replied Matilda.

'We can indeed.' replied Bertie.

'No problem, we will be in the shed.' with that Matilda, and her friends were locked up for the night.

Two days passed slowly and the clutch of hens were sad again. Eggs were gone. As darkness fell the geese, ducks and hens stood by the door becoming excited. Matilda asked everyone to be exceedingly quiet. Suddenly there was a scuffle as Sam dug a hole, whilst Bertie chewed at the wooden hinge. The door opened and all the animals left in an orderly fashion, with Bertie and Sam in the lead. They crossed the farmyard out into the field. A hungry fox looked on expectantly but didn't attack.

Across the field a somewhat frightened group arrived. It was dawn and they told their sad story to the others living on the lake. They were also refugees and made the new arrivals very welcome. Bertie and Sam left returning to the farm. In the morning the farmers thought a fox was responsible. There was a fox in the field but he was sympathetic to the animals escape to freedom. The farmyard animals made great friends with their new companions and were often visited by Bertie and Sam. Matilda thought the upheaval had been worth it, and she was very grateful to have a new life with her friends. It was a much better life for them, free from exploitation. They never did return to the farm

Matthew Gough

Story Two

Cracking Up

Dawn is breaking, first rays of sunshine peak through the bedroom window of a small, thatched farmhouse. Egbert the rooster as regular as clockwork, calls out cock-a-doodle-doos, waking the farmer and his wife reminding them to tend to their daily routines. In the farmyard open barn stands an old wooden wheeled cart once pulled by their Shire horse to gather hay, straw, and other produce from their six-acre farmland. From inside the old stable, Chic Kita, the hen with her many off spring, lift their weary heads from the cozy straw bedding, annoyed with Egbert the rooster, yet again disturbing them from their slumbering sleep. Gander the goose and the flock were also disturbed by the rooster's crowing.

'Will you shut up, every bloody morning we have this. You'll be Sunday dinner before you know it.'

'Enough of that *fowl* language', replied Egbert,

'Stop hen-dering me.'

'You are a real bad egg, aren't you? Piped up Henrietta.

'And you are a real comedy-hen.' said Egbert.

'Well you know us birds of a feather-flock together.' chirped the chickens.

Entering the stable the farmer shoos the chickens and geese out into the farmyard, carefully collecting all the freshly laid eggs, and placing them in a basket which he carried into the kitchen putting them on an old oak table. His wife was busy in the kitchen preparing the chickens' feed for the morning. He went back out and picked up his pitchfork. The farmer went over to the coop and opened it up, revealing a smelly mess. He wrinkled his nose and begun raking the manure straw out into the yard. *'What the hell has Daisy been feeding them',* he thought. He went to fetch a wheel barrow that was leaning against the wall a few feet away, and proceeded to scoop the dirty straw into the barrow with the pitchfork.

'I wonder if he will pierce his foot again.' said Henrietta.

'Yeah, remember the last time he did it? Replied Chiquita, 'we had to sleep in dirty straw for a week.'

'Didn't do my piles any good either', piped up one of the other chickens.

The chickens and geese stood around, waiting anxiously for their breakfast. Chic Kita announces to the others.

'I wonder what his wife will bring us this morning.'

'Probably popcorn.' Gander the goose replied.

'Oh no not again', replied Chiquita, 'It gets stuck in my beak.'

'Well, it might be pasta', Henrietta remarks.

'Oh, I do hope its porridge', replied Egbert.

'That stuff gets right up my nose, every time I try to eat.' remarked Chiquita.

'Well if you had a bill, you wouldn't get that problem.' laughed Ganda.

Just then they heard the kitchen door open and saw Daisy coming out with a big tray of flap jacks.

'Oh no! The last time we had those, we needed the farmer to use a sledgehammer to break them.' groaned Egbert.

The farmer, closed his eyes and shook his head, what next!

Jane Levi

Story Three

Reggie the Rampant Rooster

My last thought as the bus hit me when I crossed a busy road rushing to get to the other side. I never saw it coming. A sound like clash of cymbals. I felt myself flying at high speed through a tunnel of brilliant and flashing lights. On and on I went turning, and twisting in all shapes and sizes down this corridor of light. When will this stop where am I going?

Ahead, the tunnel widened, then another clash of cymbals accompanied by a blinding light. I woke up, it was still dark. It must have been the flash of light, half blinding me. Looking around I can see hay, and smell a faint smell of manure. I stood up, and using my arm to steady myself, I fell over. My arms? Where are they? I look to my right then my left. Dread hit me like a speeding bus *excuse the pun* I was covered in feathers.

'What the..?' I tried to say.

All that came out of my mouth, if you can call it that, were squawks and clucks. I tried to lift my arm to feel my mouth but it was so dam difficult. I lowered my head, down to my arm, *again if you can call it that* feels more like a flat stump covered in feathers. Enough I thought lets go for a walk outside. I'm beginning to get hay-fever now. I looked around. I was in some sort of farmyard. Not a soul in sight though. I looked to the horizon, and saw the sun coming up. Then something right out of my control, I couldn't help myself.

I cried out, 'Cock-a-doodle-doo.'

Well, it sounded like that and continued for five minutes. All too soon I noticed people doing chores, and suddenly out of a little door at the side of a shed a clutch of chickens marched out one by one. Must have been thirty of them? I saw a man in old fashioned clothes mucking out a stable. He was very tall but I went up to him and said.

'Excuse me, mate, I wonder if you can help me?'

All that came out of my mouth was, *'cluck, cluck, and cluck.'* A trough of water stood nearby, and I stared into the watery mirror. *Reggie, you're a goddam rooster!*

Turning around on nervous legs, an urge crept right through me. A sexual urge. Oh! I went towards the first hen and jumped on her back. Two hours later I was exhausted, and a gaggle of geese appeared, and I thought, *no, I haven't the energy*. Staggering into the hayloft, I was just in time to hear a female voice, *Ah that's more like it*, I thought and looked behind me. The maid was dressed in frilly clothes and holding a large tray of seeds which she scattered all around here and there on the ground.

Breakfast time. I'm a rooster, I'd better get used to it then.

Ade Levi

CHAPTER EIGHT

Image Eight
Story One

Hours after the Wedding

The four poster bed with crisp white sheets, a rose-pink canopy, and matching eiderdown awaited the married couple of six hours. Tobias, nineteen years, and

Henrietta barely seventeen were coupled, and the marriage agreed by their parents who were business owners. After the wedding feast family ushered Tobias, and Henrietta, into the bed chamber at the end of the great hall of his Uncle's castle where they stood separate, and silent both with their eyes embarrassingly focused toward the floor. They barely knew a thing about each other having met only once prior to the marriage. Tobias, knew he must make the first move, thus gently taking Henrietta's hand he looked at her palm predicting their future.

'You will make me a grand wife, love and care for me as your husband, and bear us both many children.' Henrietta, clutched the folds of her dress to her stomach smiling nervously. 'We cannot stand here all night Henrietta. Would you like a maid to help you undress, or do you prefer to do it yourself?'

Tobias began loosening his shoes from tired feet, and Henrietta, spotting a room screen to hide behind quickened to it preparing herself for the night. Meanwhile Tobias, in his nudity paced up and down the room until seeing Henrietta, step out naked from behind the screen both hands covering her tender parts. His manhood rose excitedly causing Henrietta, to quiver and giggle. As he approached her, suddenly a loud banging on the door startled them both.

'Tobias, I'm checking that you and, Henrietta, have all you need for this night.'
'All is fine Uncle, thank you we will see you in the morning.' The door closed behind him.
'Tobias, I'm cold!'
'It's a cold room, come let us get into bed.' he whispered.
They laid snug next to each other between the crisp white sheets their moment lacking in love.
'Are you alright Henrietta?'
'Yes, but I don't know what to do.'
'We could hug? To be honest I'm not sure what to do either. I was excited, and randy hoping things would just flow, but Uncles interruption has deflated me.'
'I'm rather tired after today's festivities Tobias, let's just

sleep.'

Daylight streaming into the bedroom through a high window woke the couple, their marriage non-consummated. As the maid brought breakfast for them on a large tray, she smiled impishly thinking of the wedding night frolics. But as she put down the tray she saw the sheets were barely crumpled, and bemused walked silently out of the room. Moments later quite agitated, and breathless after running the length of the great hall Uncle, burst into their bedroom.

'Whatever is wrong uncle?' Tobias asked.

'I've just been informed that the Justice of the Peace was an impostor! You are not legally married, and the wedding night has taken place!'

'Uncle, don't fret so no babies are on the way, and another marriage can easily be arranged next year.'

Henrietta and Tobias, not ready for marriage, smiled happily.

Gill Opal

CHAPTER NINE

the wolf asked, "you are not afraid?"

looking deep into the yellow eyes the boy replied, "I am more scared of my own kind than I will ever be of yours"

Image Nine

Story One

Escape and Reflection

Europe ripped apart by Nazi occupation, and the invasion of

Poland, resulted in several prisoner of war camps being developed with deadly consequences. Of

these notably the Krakow-Plaszow camp earned a destructive murderous reputation. Petra arrived at Plaszow as an orphan, having lost both parents, murdered by occupying Nazi forces. Thinking of her parents who were veterinary surgeons Petra, remembered her mother treating wild wolves, now a distant memory shrouded in pain and sorrow. Out in the snow fields she heard a sorrowful howling of wolves whining in sympathy for what was happening to refugee victims under the jack boot of tyranny.

Days of despair passed by absent of hope however, Petra, noticed an opening in the fence, and decided to escape. A pack of wolves close by hid her from view as they all moved slowly across the snow field toward the forest. As it began to snow the pack huddled together for warmth, and to protect Petra. Food was very scarce however, hunting in packs wolves managed to catch some prey. By this time two refugees escaped through a hole in the fence catching up with Petra, and the wolves. Gathering wood and making a fire, bits of the prey roasted in the embers tasted wonderful. The wolves made their escape through the forest accepting the three as new pack members.

The guards having found the hole in the fence dispatched patrols to search for the escapees. Wolves are excellent at concealment and camouflage, and this pack was no exception to the rule. They looked after the new pack members well. Petra was convinced the wolves had chewed a hole in the fence. She considered some of the wolves may have been treated by Petra's mother in the past. What will the three humans do next?

The journey seemingly enjoyed a purposeful route however, their destination was unknown. Days became weeks, and the guests of the pack were in good spirits. Soldiers searching the woods were wary of coming too close to the wolves, and often found themselves surrounded by the pack. As the wolves climbed to the brow of a forested hill they saw clearly down to the valley below. Lights from a farmhouse shone dimly in the distance, and the pack feeling drawn by the brightness began ambling down the hill.

Arriving at a copse of trees outside the farmhouse the pack stopped in their tracks. The pack leader wandered over to Petra. She knew instinctively their journey together was at an end. Staring deeply into the wolf's eyes Petra, intuitively felt the alpha wolf had been treated by her mother with unconditional love, and healing skills.

'I am more scared of my own kind than I will ever be with yours.' whispered Petra.

The alpha male and Petra warmly embraced, and then the pack vanished into the darkness. Petra knocked at the door. Three girls walked into a very warm kitchen. The farmer seemed to be expecting guests. In safety they remained here until liberated.

Matthew Gough

Story Two

Loki

In a small Canadian town on the edge of a vast pine forest, a young boy spent a lot of time on his own exploring the woods behind his family home. A loner, Rory, felt comfortable in the woods, nature was his friend, and he could be himself talking quietly to the wildlife. They didn't judge this boy who humans failed to understand. Late one afternoon walking the usual paths, he heard a whimpering. Drawing nearer he saw a young wolf sitting at the foot of a tree, holding a front leg aloft. Rory crouched down low for some time making eye contact with the wolf, curious to understand why this beautiful animal was crying.

Rory understood the animal was in pain needing his help. Gradually he approached the wolf as they stared at each other, and slowly a bond of trust developed. Rory sat down gently by the wolf holding out his hand. After a while a large paw landed in his small waiting palm. It was evident to Rory, the wolf had a huge thorn imbedded between his pads. He pulled the shard of wood out placing his hanky over the wound. Just like when his Mom kissed his wounds, he kissed the furry paw. Keen to share his exploits of this extraordinary event he rushed home, and straight upstairs bursting into his sister, Hanna's bedroom, puffing and stuttering.

'Rory calm down, what is this, something about a wolf? Are you making up stories again?

'He is my new best friend. He is really big, and grey with soft fur. I fixed his paw he didn't hurt me, look?'

Fishing the thorn out of his pocket he held it up proudly.

'See, I even put a bandage over his bad foot.'

Rory stuttered and anxiously shifted from foot to foot.

'You are always coming home with these wild stories little brother, there is no wolf in the woods.' Hannah replied laughing.

Over tea Rory, fidgeted his foot tapping, his head endlessly nodding. He arranged his food into three neat piles but hardly ate a mouthful.

'Gee Rory you sure are wired this afternoon honey, anything

happened at School today?' His mother asked, but knowing she would never understand the answer, avoided further discussion with the child.

The following day Rory eagerly walked the paths hoping for an encounter with his unorthodox new friend, who he named Loki. He sat at the foot of the pine tree disheartened until he felt the presence of another being. Loki appeared walking tentatively, and gently placed a pine cone at Rory's feet, backing away he sat down. Realizing his friend had bought him a gift, he grinned and without a stutter whispered clearly. 'Thank you Loki!'

For years the woods remained a wonderful sanctuary, a place of safety light, and shade, peace, and serenity. Never far away stood the distant figure strong, and loyal observing quietly through eyes familiar with the gift of kindness, and the only weakness being, of fear.

Jo Paine

Story Three

The Lonely Wolf

Once upon a time lived a very special boy. Lonely was he this young boy called Dylan. A young hermit without friends spending every day alone in the house. He did not miss the dreaded school days filled with awful memories, now behind him. Buried memories of bullying often resurfaced during nightmares, but he never remembered them when awakening.

'Indian boy', teased his school mates laughing out loud. 'What are you doing in our country? Go back to where you came from!'

Back at home, his mother tried to calm him down.

'Are you Indian?'

'No.'

'Is it true what they're saying?'

'No.'

'Then why be upset?' His mother reasoned. 'And even if you were Indian, is there anything bad about being so?'

'No!' Dylan replied.

'So why be upset?'

Still Dylan, felt unhappy, an enormous sadness as big as an ocean. Huge tears flowed down his cheeks, and Dylan never uttered a single word ever again. When he moved to another school his mum hoped things would improve. It became harder, if not impossible to get him to leave the house in the mornings. On the first day his mother told the new teacher not to expect Dylan, to speak too much as he was very shy. Two weeks later Dylan's mother, asked the teacher how he was getting along. The teacher agreed.

'You are right Dylan, doesn't speak. In fact we have two other boys just like him, and both are on the autistic spectrum. Unfortunately, the other boys tend to pick on them but we'll do what we can to protect him.'

The school was near Dylan's home across the green by the

hill, and he was just starting to walk there, and back home all by himself. One afternoon however, Dylan, did not arrive back home. His mother sat in the kitchen staring at the clock when a loud knock, and the sound of children's agitated voices disturbed her. Opening the door three boys spoke at once.

'The big boys surrounded Dylan, and beat him up! They all ganged up surrounding Dylan, beating him very badly! We watched as he ran away to hide up the hill. We tried to find him but couldn't!

Dylan's mother, in a panic left the house immediately to search for him. She searched everywhere but he was nowhere to be seen. She decided to look up the hill. Heart in her mouth, she saw a runner coming down the slope, and begged him.

'My son has been injured, please help me find him.'

The runner ran back up the hill, and found Dylan, hiding behind a tree. From this day onward Dylan, never went outside, refusing to leave the house again. Finding refuge in a virtual world he loved playing his favorite game, *'The Last Wolf.'* One day the wolf asked him.

'You seem not afraid?'

Looking deep into large yellow eyes the boy replied.
'I am more scared of my own kind than I will ever be of yours.'

Paula Jardim

CHAPTER TEN

**Image Ten
Story One**

Keeping Watch at Craig y Nos Castle.

Early in the nineteenth century on a small working farm nestled under the Sleeping Giant, near Ystradgynlais, lived Gwen, Richard, and their son Dai. It was an idyllic existence, and sheep farming was very profitable at this time. All appeared to be well in the garden, and Dai attended the local school where his studies were going well. His ambition was to be a doctor. Whilst undertaking the routine of preparing the sheep for market Gwen, fell sustaining a small laceration. Thinking nothing more about it sadly her arm became infected with sepsis. Richard, and Dai, were both devastated when Gwen passed away. He was looking forward to his auntie coming to stay at the farm to help out during this traumatic time. Dai became very depressed and unwell with a persistent cough. It was annoying at first but gradually became chronic, and after a while Mycobacterium Tuberculosis was diagnosed as pleurisy developed.

It was agreed with the doctor a period of convalescence at Craig- y- Nos Castle was needed. At this time the Castle was a sanatorium purporting to provide effective treatment. But Dai, developed pneumonia with respiratory arrest becoming very frail, and despite Richard and the medical staff's best efforts, Dai passed away. It was such a tragedy, and Richard became very distraught at the funeral. Craig y Nos became a place of great sorrow as death followed tragic death.

Dai's, metaphysical being departed leaving his body. He was aware of his surroundings endlessly walking corridors in the castle. Eventually finding the operatic theatre, he recalled how his mother Gwen would often watch theatrical productions staged there. Dai felt he would really like to see his mother again, and with a form of telekinesis wished for this to happen. He was aware there were other spirits living in Craig y Nos, all of which sought eternal rest. When he found a front bedroom on the second floor Dai, kept watch, waiting to see a glimpse of his mother Gwen.

Dai waited for several nights, and often could be seen by onlookers looking out the bedroom window all night long until dawn. On the final night before a full moon, a strange eerie fog swirled around the grounds of Craig y Nos, covering the trees in a shimmering shroud of iridescent light.

Dai, was ecstatic at the sight of his mother as Gwen's, metaphysical being walked towards him. Their spirits greeted in embrace, and a bright light beam entwined them both bringing peace and quiescence. An unbelievably peaceful resonance radiated throughout every inch of Craig y Nos on this night. Dai, and Gwen, wandered together arm in arm toward the theatre. They fondly remembered the past concerts with such happiness and joy, indeed one could almost hear music and festivities.

An operatic resonance filled the theatre. Suddenly, a huge flash of light filled the space and Dai, and Gwen, disappeared. A host of phantom wanderers still inhabit Craig- y- Nos forever haunted by its vibrant colorful history.

Matthew Gough

CHAPTER ELEVEN

Image Eleven
Story One

The Bard's Visit

On the hillside young Dafydd, had been tending the sheep when he suddenly looked out to sea shielding blinded eyes from the direct sunlight. In the distance he could see a white sail, a boat heading directly to the harbour. He heard the Poet Iolo Gogh, was travelling through the villages of West Wales, from the North coast where he lived. He had heard about this from the preacher who had impressed upon the congregation to listen to the Bard, if ever he was to visit their village. Dafydd ran along the cliff edge, keeping the boat in sight, as he headed toward the small hamlet where he lived with his Mam, Dad, brothers and sisters. As he ran, he shouted out.

'Quickly, Iolo the Bard is arriving, get ready, make haste!'

At the sight of his young son running along the cliff edge

shouting, Mr. Thomas, instructed his wife to get ready, and bring the children to the oak tree where local people often gathered to hear the preacher speak words of wisdom on fine days. It didn't take long before word spread, and families gathered, old women embracing grandchildren, nursing mothers, husbands, and their children. Even Betty, often teased by the small children, who spent her days looking after the pigs, and Mary who hastened from the nearby stream still in a state of semi-dress, carrying a pitcher of water in readiness for the Bard's arrival.

Old men struggled up the hill to the story-telling tree, walking sticks firmly in hand, and eager to hear the melodious timbre from the famous Bard. Young parents were eager their children should witness this very special, and unique occasion.

Iolo Goch arrived, red cape around his shoulders with distinctive grey hair and beard, carrying a harp. He greeted the villagers who sat eagerly around him awaiting the spoken word flowing so eloquently from his mouth like a mountain stream. He expressed his support for the Nobleman Owain Glendower, in a poem dedicated to his honour, and to the great house in North Wales. Iolo played the harp, and the audience hushed with deep respect and piety. Never before had they heard such wonderful poetry, which to them was strange and haunting, and full of praise. His words even attracted ducks, hens, and the cows from the fields to hear his musical tones, and booming voice. Babies and children were spellbound as if by magic. The older villagers eager to hear of the friendship between Iolo Gogh, and Owain Glendower, beamed with patriotic pride.

As the recital came to an end Iolo, drank deeply from the pitcher of fresh spring water, and was invited to sit, and take food with the villagers. It was such a great honour for them to have the famous Bard amongst them. Iolo was as much at home with humble country people as he was with the Welsh nobility, even kings. The day at last ended, and Iolo bade everyone farewell, resuming his journey across Wales.

Rosalind Gough

Story Two
Under The Old Oak Tree

Born in 1320, Iolo Goch a medieval Welsh bard composed cywyddau (a unique form of poetry) and elegy for lords, noblemen, and even kings. Three of his poems honored the life of Owain Glyndwr. In one, he describes Glyndwr's home, Sycharth Castle, with the main house, many outbuildings of impressive construction, and its extensive estate, fishpond, dovecotes, a mill, deer park, rabbit warrens, all surrounded by golden hayfields. He praised the generosity of Glyndwr, for providing grand banquets, and fine wines lavished upon his guests. Iolo Goch rented a small portion of his family's ancient patrimony in the township of Llewenni where he possessed a house.

An old oak tree stands on one side of a river with a huge broken branch disabled from its trunk, where a small bird perches almost every day chirping the sweet sound of birdsong Every Sunday, Iolo, wearing his bard's robes and cowhide leather boots sits comfortably under the oak tree. Whilst playing the harp he recites descriptive poems and cywyddau to audiences of castle maids, servants, local villagers, and their children. Many folk travel from far and wide, and then relax listening attentively to the recitations. A maid carries an earthenware jug pouring wine into a silver chalice for refreshment as he sips between poems. Children were always engrossed by his descriptive poems praising animals, livestock, and the wildlife inhabiting Glyndwr's estate.

Iolo was well aware of difficulties between the English and Welsh, but at this time Owain Glyndwr and his brother Tudur fought alongside Richard II of England in many campaigns. Iolo continued with his writings and compositions performing to Lords, gentry, and loyal audiences across Wales. Iolo recalled the time when he sat under an old oak, when Bronwyn, the farmer's daughter carried a large earthenware jug filled to the brim with elderberry wine. It was a very funny turn of events making him laugh so hard tears rolled down his face. She had just woken up after a busy day tending crops in the fields, scything hay, and gathering it into trusses. Bronwyn's little brother excitedly shouted Iolo Goch, had returned from his visits around the country. Quickly Bronwyn, jumped out of bed still in her night gown, and rushed outside to the outhouse. Reaching for the earthenware jug containing a gallon of elderberry wine she brewed two months ago, she held it in her arms.

Still dressed in her nightgown and bare foot, she ran up the path toward where Iolo Gogh was entertaining the children and villagers. The broken branch of the old oak tree jutted out from the side of the path, and Bronwyn tripped over it. The earthenware jug flew into the air out of her hands, drenching her from head to toe. She stood up, the white night gown now pink, her blonde hair turning a reddish color. She hobbled over to Iolo and apologized. He was so amused, and in between hysterical laughter he thought to himself, *now there's a poem I can write.*

Jane Levi

Story Three

The Seer

He appeared almost overnight carrying nothing but a tiny wooden stool, and a small lyre wrapped in a brilliant azure blanket. The herdsman taking his flock to the meadow was the first to notice him. He wandered over to the aged man, and asked *would he like to partake of some of the bread, cheese, and mead he had with him.* The ancient man's eyes were of cold-blue-ice seeing naught but noticing all. He spoke in a language unknown which sounded like gibberish to the herdsman. Disconcerted, and with a sense of uneasiness the herdsman bade fare well to the stranger, and followed his grazing cattle.

As the villagers started their new day more interest was shown, children hung back at a distance their curiosity conflicting with fear. The blacksmith of the village stopped his duties tempted toward by the guttural sounds. A tanner deserted his half prepared hides drying in the sun, eager to witness the strange spectacle. By the time the sun reached its zenith a small crowd had gathered around the visionary. Young children sat at his feet, and a few of the villagers looked on in bemusement, curiosity, and awe. A woman of the village gave an offering of mead pouring it into a silver chalice. Even the nesting birds deserted their eggs to observe what was occurring below.

A strange new feeling hung in the haze. Emotions were checked, and the villagers spoke in hushed tones. A stranger had appeared whose unseeing eyes saw all. By dusk the mood had turned, children refused to return to their homes, milk-laden cows were restless, impatient, and their cries of discomfort echoed across the vale. Bouts of speaking in tongues broke the madness of silence yet the worshippers of the visionary seemed to understand every word. As night approached the mood became ugly, and villagers were clearly divided into followers, and the non-believers.

Hostility soon grew, and in their rage some tried to drive

the stranger away. He wasn't welcome here they cried. He wasn't of this village, and now he must go. The stranger sat steadfast, and one by one they left frustrated returning to the safety of their homes. Only the children remained. Let them stay there, the villagers agreed, they'll soon come home. As the cold unforgiving moon slowly ascended the night sky, the villagers in their beds could hear faint sounds of a lyre being plucked. Melancholy, yearning, and a deep sense of loss seeped like a thief into their dreams.

Now it was morning, and the start of a new day. As if controlled by one single thought the villagers quickly made their way to the old oak tree where the stranger had held court the day before. He was gone, and so were the children. The air was full of loss, and the villagers were frightened, for all that remained was a slight indentation on the dew-soaked grass where his stool had been, and blackened bare patches where the children once sat.

Holly Morgan

CHAPTER TWELVE

**Image Twelve
Story One**

Apples in the Air

During the early part of the 18th century in Eastern Europe there was a small house on a cobbled street. Wisps of wood smoke rose from the chimney, and fluttered in the breeze. It was autumn, and dry leaves lay everywhere on the street. The lady of the house started to

brew tea for Jack, who often popped in for a cup. He lived 5 doors away down the street. Jack was very excited about the circus coming to his town, and he adored juggling. One day he dreamed,

I might join a circus. For several days Jack, looked through the fence and wondered what kind of circus it would be. Would the ring master let jack juggle, he hoped he would? *Goodness it's time for tea,* and with that Jack, ran down the street passing his own home where tea was being prepared.

Tea was brewing on the hearth, and the lady was fast asleep. Jack without thinking started to juggle three apples, and was doing very well then he included a fourth, it was brilliant. All the apples danced in the air when suddenly one fell dropping on a plate. It smashed to the floor. The lady awoke startled, and saw the plate in several pieces, apples on the floor. Jack was feeling very guilty.

The broken crockery was a relic from Russian history in the time of the Czars. This plate was a piece from the late Catherine the Great's collection, and was passed down by her great uncle. The lady described its history to Jack, pointing to the collection, and saying where it came from. Jack was determined to replace the plate but how? With that they both had tea.

'A new plate will be available upon my return.' he said, a promise held in great doubt by the lady.

Jack arrived at the circus with four apples, and before the ringmaster could say, *'Get out of my circus'* the juggling act began. Four apples were juggled, then a fifth and a sixth, all danced in the air. The crowd were ecstatic, and very appreciative of the act. When the performance came to an end Jack, holding several apples took a bow, and left the ring. He was greeted by a lady who *appeared from nowhere* and, in a very strong voice said.

'Jack take this plate in gratitude of your performance, and recognition of your future circus career. Keep an eye out, for I will guide you. I was given this plate by the custodian of Catherine's treasure who made me promise to hand it to a deserving promising lad. You have been chosen as that young lad.'

With that the lady disappeared in a flash leaving the plate

behind. Jack ran to the house and handed it to the lady. Tears of joy filled the room, and the plate joined the collection as promised. Jack went on to have a successful circus career enjoying tutoring from the mysterious lady. The lady of the house often visited the circus.

Matthew Gough

Story Two

The Orchard

Gustav often glanced across the dirt path track from his bedroom window admiring the flourishing orchard, full of red apples, pear trees, and small fruit bushes. They were a poor family. Gustav, and his mother lived in a tiny stone-cold cottage with only the bare essentials. His father passed away with tuberculosis two years ago. His mother found it very difficult to make ends meet.

One day after school three of Gustav's friends suggested they steal apples from the orchard. Gustav with his shy mild-mannered ways thought this was not a good idea. But not wishing to look like a coward in his friends' eyes, went along with the plan. They crept quietly into the orchard trampling over blackberry bushes until they reached the apple tree at the back of the orchard. An abundance of red rosy apples adorned the tree. Pulling down branches, and shaking them vigorously many apples fell on to the ground. The boys filled their pockets with as many as they possibly could. Suddenly they heard footsteps, and a disgruntled voice, it was the gardener coming into the orchard.

'Come here you little beggars. Those are not for you to steal. They are for me to sell at the market for the old woman.'

Surprised and scared the boys ran off, apples falling to the ground one by one from overfull pockets. Gustav being far slower than his friends was left behind as they disappeared over the orchard wall. The gardener caught the boy by the scruff of the neck, gripping him tightly by the collar. He marched Gustav forcefully to the old woman's cottage with apples still bulging in his pockets.

The old woman glanced up from her knitting, startled by the commotion in the garden outside. The kitchen door opened, there stood her gardener restraining the young boy by the collar, feet dangling in the air, when stolen apples tumbled to the stone floor. One apple bounced on the table shattering a dish into pieces.

'What have we here then?' the old woman asked sternly.

'I discovered young boys, pinching apples from your apple trees, trampling bushes and causing damage. The others ran off but I caught this one.' Gustav wriggled under the gardeners grasp.

Gustav protested trying to get free.

'I only wanted to pick some apples for my mother to make an apple pie, we are so poor, and an apple pie would be so delicious.'

The old woman felt very sorry for Gustav and calmly said.

'I will make your mother one of my special apple pies but first you can clean the floor, and pick up those apples.'

Gustav did as asked, and watched as the old woman rolled pastry on a floured board adding apples, topping it with a pastry lid. Later she placed the cooked pie carefully on a favorite blue porcelain plate. Gustav apologized profusely thanking the old woman for her kindness. After this she continued to bake an apple pie every week for Gustav and his mother.

Jane Levi

Story Three

Marco

Marco ran so fast, heart beating like a drum thumping against his rib cage. Pounding of the bigger boys feet echoed behind him, if caught he would get a beating but Marco was fast as the wind and soon reached the safety of the farmstead. Bracing both hands on bent knees gasping breath back into empty lungs Marco paused momentarily, before entering the stone cottage where the old woman sat dozing. Slowly Marco reached up to steal an apple and at that very second Nona awoke.

'Marco!' she screamed.

Startled he stepped back, the plate crashed to the stone floor, apples rolled here and there, he froze.

'What are you doing coming in here stealing, you could ask child?' she said.

'Sorry Nona' his head bowed

'Go and help your father in the fields'.

Marco crashed through the farmyard, chickens leapt in the air, feathers flapping, clucking loudly with disgust. Down to the cut corn fields he ran, it was like running on a golden silk river.

'Papa, papa.' he called holding a hat between nimble fingers.

In the distance stood father shielding his eyes from the afternoon sun. Marco ran to him grasping tightly round his strong legs.

'Marco my boy, you have come to see your father at last.' he joked. 'Tell me have you been behaving yourself?'

Marco nodded his face still buried in his father's legs.

'Go and see to Arturo, take him back up with you and feed him.'

As the boy turned moving slowly towards a donkey under a tree, father shook his head. He knew the boy was getting into trouble and made a promise to himself to spend more time with him.

'Eh, Matteo.' One of the itinerant workers called to him. 'You coming for a drink'

Matteo envied them their carefree lives, he should have got away from the village when he had the chance as a young man, but instead he chose love. As he walked back from the village he felt crunching of dry leaves underfoot, walnuts scattered the path along with lemons and ripe sticky figs. Heavy scents filled the air and Matteo was transported back to the night he and Rosa married. The village all danced under the moonlight. He could see her now twirling round dancing with jet black hair tumblingdown to her waist, beautiful dark eyes with cherry like lips red and luscious.

She came to Matteo in dreams until he woke, when his heart would sink heavily into his chest with a stark cruel reality. He was sitting in his chair when Marco climbed down the wooden ladder from the loft above and without speaking, clambered on to his father's lap. The child was so like Rosa it hurt.

'Tomorrow my boy we are going to Verona.' the boy's eyes shone with excitement.

'Papa we will be up with the lark, I will brush Arturo until he gleams.'

His father pulled him closer.

'I know son, you will make your mamma proud.'

Jo Paine

IMAGES

1. Failing Memories – Charles Spence Layh (1865-1958)
2. Man leaning on Bar with Dog – Norman Cornish (1919-2014)
3. The Apothecary – Vidor Cabor (1937-1999)
4. Stairway to Heaven – Hans Bulder (1953)
5. Salem – Sydney Curnow Vosper (1866-1942)
6. Dr. Zahi & Sarcophagus of Hekashepes (2023)
7. The Poultry Meal - Marie-Francois Firmin Girard (1838-1921)
8. Arnolfini Portrait – Jan Van Eyck (1390-1441)
9. Wolf and Boy – Image - North American Indian Quote
10. Craig-y-Nos Castle – Image – Most Haunted Castle in Wales
11. Iolo Goch – Arwr-yr-Eryod – Andrew Asser (2010)
12. Grandmother's Reprimand – Michelle Cammarano (1835-1920)

Ystradgynlais Creative Writing Group

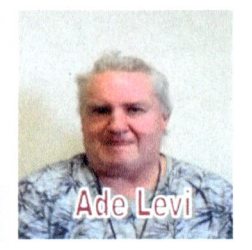

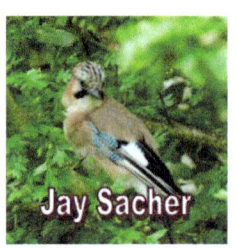

- Rosalind Mary Gough
- Paula Jardin
- Matthew Gough
- Jane Levi
- Gill Opal
- Ade Levi
- Holly Morgan
- Jo Paine
- Jay Sacher
- Meiriona Davies
- Lazarus Carpenter

SWIFT ARROW BOOKS